"Man, this book is good! It's very gripping, and the imagery is spectacular...Wow!" ~ B.W.

"I'm definitely intrigued, this book is needed. It will help people who have gone through abuse, and also help others to understand the victims of abuse. It's heart wrenching and powerful!" ~ R.C.

"I'm extremely inspired! This book makes me feel like I am right there with Layla. The author did a good job painting a very clear and vivid picture." ~ S.D.

"It's an engaging and touching story! This book invites the reader to perceive the trauma and pain of people needing comfort, deliverance, and healing. I believe this book is going to help a lot of people." ~ M.R.

MY  Grace

IS SUFFICIENT

God's Strength Is Made Perfect in Weakness

MEGAN WALKER

WESTBOW
PRESS®
A DIVISION OF THOMAS NELSON
& ZONDERVAN

WestBow Press books may be ordered through booksellers or by contacting:

WestBow Press
A Division of Thomas Nelson & Zondervan
1663 Liberty Drive
Bloomington, IN 47403
www.westbowpress.com
1 (866) 928-1240

ISBN: 978-1-9736-5156-7 (sc)
ISBN: 978-1-9736-5155-0 (hc)
ISBN: 978-1-9736-5157-4 (e)

Library of Congress Control Number: 2019900543

Print information available on the last page.

WestBow Press rev. date: 03/12/2019

THANK YOU

To my Lord and Savior Jesus Christ,
my natural family, my church family, my
friends, and everyone that helped me in any
way to write and/or publish this book.

Thank you for every prayer, every encouraging
word, every monetary contribution, and every
review. I could not have done this without you.

Your love and support has meant so much to
me. You are such a huge blessing, and I thank
God for you more than you may ever know!

DEDICATION

To the millions of people who are struggling
with the pain and misery of abuse, or seemingly
hopeless situations...**there is hope!**

CONTENTS

INTRODUCTION

Sometimes in life, difficult situations will arise, and we may find ourselves questioning God. I'm not talking about, "I have a headache today, God why do I have to have a headache?" and I'm not talking about, "My feelings are hurt, God why does my feelings have to be hurt?"

I'm talking about the kind of difficulty that doesn't just hurt you, but crushes you. I'm talking about the kind of pain that hurts so bad, and stays so long that you just become numb.

People all over the world are faced with numbing hurt every day. The kind of pain that will make a person say, "I just don't know what to do. I can't do this. I can't make it. I can't go on, this is too much. I feel like I'm suffocating. I just want to die."

Recent news stories tell us that many people would rather die, than to go through what they are facing. Some people attempt suicide, and some succeed. Some people go on a rampage in an effort to hurt others, and some just hurt in hopes that someday things will change for the good. Someday it will all be over.

Here is what I love about God during life's challenges. In 2 Corinthians 12:9, He informed Paul that His grace is sufficient! He said, "For my power is made perfect in weakness."

This means, whatever you are going through, God is yet there, He has full control. Your struggle was not allowed just to make you weak, but to strengthen you. It hasn't been allowed to take you out, but to bring you in. Neither has it been allowed to destroy you, but to make you. The Grace of God is more than enough for you.

My Grace is Sufficient!

Everything that God allows is for a purpose. We don't always know what that purpose is, but God knows. We don't always understand, but God does. We can't always see our way out, but God can. We were formed in the womb for a specific purpose. So then, everything that we face in this life builds and prepares us for the purpose that God has for us. Nothing that we go through is pointless-it all works together for our good.

My Grace is Sufficient!

In this book, we take a look at the life of a young girl named Layla Martin, who persevered through a number of tough situations. She was hurt, abused, and felt as if she had no reason to live. Day after day, year after year; there was hurt after hurt. Crushing and debilitating hurt-of which she could see no way out. Until of course, she surrendered her life to God.

My Grace is Sufficient!
2 Corinthians 12:9

A SNAPSHOT

Stop! Please stop Momma!

I'm sorry! Please Stop!

What did I do that was this bad?"

Those were the thoughts that raced through Layla's mind as her mother fought her. This happened often, but Layla never fought back. She was afraid that fighting back; or saying anything, would only make things worse. Layla didn't want revenge. She loved her mother, and only wanted her to stop.

Along with the physical abuse, Layla's mother would cuss her out completely; calling her every name that a person might want to call their worst enemy, but certainly not their daughter.

As Layla grew older, she began to realize, that most of what her mother did; was not necessarily things that she could control on her own. Her mother acted according to what was in her. Negative was going in, so surely negative is what was coming out.

Layla- feeling her way through life; quickly began to indulge in a number of adult behaviors. All of which, were approved, accepted, introduced, and encouraged by her mother. The lifestyle that so many adults were living around her became the lifestyle that seemed normal.

Layla's mother used her often to get what she wanted- usually money and drugs. She was focused on getting the next high, and was willing to do whatever it took to get there. Even if it meant, giving her daughter in exchange.

Chapter One

A PRISON OF
SILENCE

"Y ou get on my nerves. I hate kids!"
"You can't even do something so simple."
"Get out of my face!"
Layla's mother yelled angrily.

Layla didn't move as fast as her mother wanted her to, so she took her fist and punched her in the face causing her to fall. When she hit the floor, her mother started kicking her and cussing her out.

When she was finished, she said, "Get up and move out of my way!"

Layla looked up at the coffee table that was right next to her. She placed her hand on top of the table, and used it to pull herself up off of the floor.

She went to her room, while her mother sat at the table and smoked a joint.

The next day; while walking to the store, Layla ran into Chris- a boy that lived in the neighborhood.

"What happened to your eye? Layla, you been fighting?" asked Chris.

"No, I fell and hit my face on the table." Layla replied.

Looking confused, Chris said, "Mmmm, you fell pretty hard, didn't you?"

"Yea, but I'll be alright. It'll go away soon." said Layla."

She changed the subject, and the two of them continued walking to the store.

There is a major difference between chastising someone because you love them, & just down right abuse. Layla's mother fought her all the time. She had many black eyes, busted lips, and bruises anywhere on her body. Other children would ask her about it, but she would find a way to cover it up.

While school was in session, her teachers and counselors didn't notice anything suspicious. Layla was well kept, and never really appeared "needy". She was quiet-for the most part, respectful, managed to make really good grades, and didn't get in any trouble. She had her share of fights, but only when someone bothered her.

Layla began drinking alcohol before she was ten years old. She liked to drink, because her mother thought it was cute. It made her mother happy to see Layla doing things that she did. It was like their time to bond. Her mother didn't mind going to get alcohol for her, and allowing her to drink at home. If Layla had friends over, she didn't mind them drinking either. They would sit and drink until they just couldn't take anymore, or until it was all gone. The parents of those other children had no idea what was going on while their children were away.

"I'm hungry, what are we going to eat?" Layla asked her older brother.

"I don't know!" her brother replied.

"Where is Momma? We haven't seen her in a couple of days!" Layla thought.

"How could she leave us here and not care if we have eaten or not?"

From the outside looking in, it seemed that everything was fine at home, but that wasn't the case.

Layla liked to be to herself. She never really enjoyed being outside, and although she had a number of friends, her favorite place to be was alone in her room. It was where she felt safe. It was where she found peace.

In the back of Layla's mind, she knew that there was more to life than what she had been experiencing; she just didn't know if she would ever be able to live that life.

Whenever Layla didn't do things that her mother wanted her to do, she would threaten her by saying that she was going to send her to the home for black children. Of course, as a child, Layla feared being sent to such a place; but she often thought, "In all actuality, being a foster child, or in a group home, may be a better place to be."

She felt that way then, but she looks back on life now, and rejoices in The Lord for not being removed from the situation too soon. The Lord blessed her to go through it, and she's forever grateful.

Layla worked hard to please her mother. She just wanted to make her happy.

She just wanted to do something right.

It was her goal.

No matter how hard Layla tried, her mother never seemed happy. She continued to beat and cuss Layla out anyway.

Layla got tired of it, and there was only so much more that she could stand. The love that she once had; turned into hatred, and she couldn't stand to be around her mother anymore. Layla began to be upset every time her mother acted like she loved and cared about her, because in her heart, she knew that she really didn't.

Things had gotten so bad that Layla was literally trying to figure out how she could do away with her mother for good.

She wanted her mother gone.

She wanted her dead, because she felt like her mother was slowly killing her.

The devil started making her believe that the only way out was death. That meant somebody would have to die. It was either going to be Layla or her Mother. Layla thought, "If I don't kill her, she's going to continue to slowly kill me and make me suffer!"

She was fed up. She was tired, and she just wanted it to be over. Thankfully, the Lord always somehow intervened, and did not allow Layla to carry out those plans to kill her mother.

Layla's heart turned cold to everyone around her, especially close relatives. She felt that no one was brave enough to take her and her brother out of her mother's care. She thought,

"They don't love us, they don't care!
If they did, they would help us!"

For many years, Layla didn't know who her father was, and her grandmother lived in another state. So she couldn't always run to either of them for help. However, once her grandmother moved back home, Layla stayed with her as much as her mother would allow. She was able to stay for extended amounts of time, but whenever her mother decided to disrupt things; she would come cussing and fussing, demanding that Layla return home with her immediately.

One afternoon, Layla's mother was upset about something that had nothing to do with Layla, but she took her anger and frustration out on her. She beat Layla badly; once again, punching her in the face, knocking her to the ground, and kicking her all over her body.

She did not stop until Layla began to have an asthma attack. Panting for air, Layla said,

"I can't breathe!"

"I can't breathe!"

"I can't breathe!"

So her mother stopped. Immediately after she stopped, she looked at Layla and said, "I'm not taking you to the hospital either!"

Then she walked to the liquor store to buy a drink. There were a few relatives nearby, they had compassion and decided to take Layla to the hospital. They all got in the truck, and drove right past her mother- who was still walking to the liquor store. With an evil countenance, she looked at the truck and showed no concern.

When Layla made it to the hospital, she had visible bruises all over her body, and the doctors mentioned that she seemed very upset. While the doctor was out of the room, her mother called. Filled with guilt, she bribed Layla. She said all the right things so that Layla wouldn't tell the doctors what really happened.

"Layla, how are you doing?" Her mother asked.

"I'm ok." Layla responded.

"You're gonna be alright. I need you to get better, and be able to leave out of there." Her mother said.

Layla sat on the phone quietly.

Her mother recognized the silence; then she said, "I love you!"

Layla responded, "I love you too." Then she passed the phone back to those who were with her.

Layla couldn't believe what was happening. Just before her mother called, she was ready to tell everything that was going on. She was devastated! But after talking to her mother, she was afraid to say anything. She convinced herself that her mother wasn't going to beat her anymore.

Layla lived most of her young life fearful of
what her Mother would do to her. It seemed that
her mother didn't beat her because she was a bad
child, but because she wasn't bad enough.

It was like Layla's mother would rather for her
to hit her back, or cuss her out-then she would
be normal. Layla never retaliated in such a way
though, and it seemed as if her mother hated her
more because she didn't.

Layla's mother didn't hate her, but the spirits
working in her mother did. Everything that they
tried to do to defeat Layla didn't work though. God
had His hands on that girl from the very beginning.
She was just too young to fully understand.

Abuse was prevalent in Layla's life, including:
sexual, verbal, physical, and emotional. This
resulted in evil spirits being deposited in and
attached to her. She was doing things that no adult
should do, let alone a child. She became filled with
spirits of: confusion, hurt, and fear. She was on the
devil's hit list, but no matter what happened and
how bad things got, The Lord wouldn't allow the
devil to take her life.

Things only seemed to become more severe,
and Layla often wondered why she was still alive.
She held on though, believing that it couldn't
possibly be an accident. She had enough sense

to know that all she had been through could've taken her life, or caused her to become mentally ill. She was still alive though, and functioning as if everything was ok. She couldn't quite put it all together in her mind, but she knew that there was a purpose for her life.

During this time, Layla didn't know the Lord. She hardly ever went to church, but it was something holding her up. She had strength all along.

She may not have known the Lord, but He surely did know her. He was showing her that He loved her more than anyone else ever could.

Abandonment and neglect were two things that the enemy used to set Layla up. He had plans to destroy her life before it ever really began. He wanted her, and he wanted her badly. He knew that if she ever really came into the knowledge and the love of God, she would be a threat to his kingdom.

Author's Note: **Reader, please understand the fight for our lives is real. The enemy comes to steal, kill, and destroy! It doesn't just happen at a "certain point" of a person's life, rather the devil's traps, plans, and snares start from the very beginning of life. Genesis 50:20 NIV says, you intended to harm me, but God**

intended it for good, to accomplish what is now being done, the saving of many lives.

Everything that the devil tried to do in an effort to send Layla to hell only pushed her closer to God, in an amazingly awesome way! She became hungry and thirsty for the Lord's righteousness, and began to go after Him all she knew how- praying and pleading with God for help, deliverance, and more of Him.

Blessed are they which do hunger and thirst after righteousness: for they shall be filled. -Matthew 5:6

Chapter Two

SOMETHING'S GOTTA GIVE

round the clock, anytime, and anywhere; the abuse continued. From pulling Layla's hair, to punching her in the face, choking her, and beating her up, then leaving her in the closet alone. The physical abuse was extensive and intense.

Often times, the verbal abuse served as the pre-requisite for what was to come-the physical abuse.

It wasn't too many instances where Layla was cussed out, and then it was done. Her mother almost always accompanied it with some sort of physical abuse. It was expected.

She loved backing Layla up into a wall or a

corner, so that she had no way out. She was very good at it too. Cussing and name calling for countless minutes before Layla would find herself backed into a corner. She would put her finger in Layla's face and be so close to her yelling that she could smell the drugs and alcohol on her mother's breath, and see the white foaming spit filling in her mouth as she spoke. Naturally, Layla would back up. Not only was she afraid, she didn't want all of that in her face. Every time she backed up, her mother moved forward, and before she knew it, she was trapped.

It was then that her mother would take her fist, swing and hit Layla with all of her might-holding nothing back, no reservation at all. She was hitting to hurt, hitting to kill! Layla had so much respect for her mother that she never hit her back or even argued with her. Sure enough, it definitely crossed Layla's mind as she got older, but she thought, "What will that solve?" She had enough sense to know that it would most likely only make things worse.

Layla endured so many episodes of abuse that it would be almost impossible to cram all of them into one book. In March of 2016, Layla agreed to take part in an interview with Samantha, a very good friend of hers. Samantha watched Layla struggle for years, dealing with the trauma of all that happened to her. She figured that an interview would at least help Layla to reflect, and verbally release what she had bottled inside for so long. Here are some portions of that interview below:

Samantha: You mentioned that your Mother gave you some black eyes, busted noses, and things of that nature; what do you remember about her beating you? When would she do it? Was it always at night?

Layla: No! It was all of the time; it could be early in the morning before I got on the school bus. It could be in the middle of the day; or right after school. Ummm, on a Saturday, a Sunday, late in the middle of the night, whenever!

I believe this happened, because there was never a specific time that she wasn't smoking or drinking. Sometimes she would wake up high or drunk from the night before. Or she would have a hangover and be upset, so of course, that wouldn't help the situation. The only time that she appeared to be really calm, was when I guess she would hit a certain high. If she was anything less than that highest feeling that she felt like she could feel, she was angry. I could tell the "level" she was on just by talking to her on the phone.

There were certain "levels" that would

determine the severity of her actions, most of the time. She had a level where she would be under the influence of something, but she was angry. That meant that she hadn't gotten "enough". She needed some more of whatever it was that she was currently on: the drugs, alcohol, or both.

There was another "level" where she would just be "up there," in the clouds, calm, and it seemed that nothing was bothering her. During those times, she would say things like, "It's all good baby!" and I'd know that she was trippin.

If she wasn't "there", she was mad, frustrated, and wrestling. As a child I felt like she was crazy and out of her whole mind.

Samantha: Were you the only child in the home being abused?

Layla: Absolutely not! My older brother was there, I never felt like he got the same treatment. I soon realized that he chose a different approach to deal with it though. It seemed like he was in trouble at home a lot, but I would get punished for it. That was always difficult for me to understand.

Samantha: What do you mean by "punished for what he did wrong?"

Layla: One evening I was in my room just minding my business when my brother came home.

My mother was upset with him about something, so she began to cuss him out.

Now, my brother didn't have a whole lot of respect for her, and he was not someone that would just let her do anything to him. He would argue with her when she began to cuss him out. It was hard for her to "get a good grip" on him because he was not only her son, but also one of her drug suppliers. He lived at home, but was allowed to continue his street life as long as he kept her happy. So, if he didn't give her drugs and money, she would take it from him. Naturally, that made him upset and he lost respect for her.

This particular night when they were arguing, she became extremely upset, and began to fight him.

Oh My!

He began to fight her back, and why did he do that? She carried a razor blade often; she whipped out the razor blade and began to slice him across the back of his neck. He was furious! When he was able to get her off of him, he continued cussing her out while running out the door.

Once she realized that she couldn't catch him, she was extremely mad! Her focus shifted and she came raging in my room saying,

"And I'm sick of you too!"

Confused and standing there near the closet, I wondered, "What did I do?"

She just began to hit me in the face and upper body. Hitting hard enough to knock me into the closet. Even after knocking me in the closet, she continued to beat me. Kicking and punching me everywhere.

No mercy!

I had a fresh pin-curl hair style, with lots of closed bobby pins, and spritz that she pulled apart by hand.

Wow, that was so painful! I can still feel it when I think about it.

She loved to hit me in my face and pull my hair. After she had enough, she left me alone in the closet: bruised, bleeding, and sore.

Most of all, I was devastated and heartbroken. Eventually, I peeled myself off of the floor, cleaned myself up, and got in the bed.

Samantha: WOW! WOW! WOW! Was this the worse that she did?

Layla: No, not at all! There was another situation when I was home with a friend of mine and I hadn't seen my mother in a day or so. She had a male friend stop by to see her, and I told him that I would let her know that he stopped by.

Well, being human, I forgot to tell her and about a month had passed.

I was staying the night at someone else's house. My mother showed up with the male friend that had come by the house a month before. It was fairly late, and I remember being just about sleep when she knocked on the window really hard.

In her profane language, she angrily said, "Come outside now!"

"Yea, you got the game twisted!"

So nervous and not sure what this was about, I went outside. She said,

"Get in the car!"

She got in the backseat on the passenger's side, and told me to get in the front seat; while her male friend was sitting in the driver's seat.

Pointing to the guy, she said,

"He told me that he came by to see me a while ago, and he told you to let me know that he came by. I didn't know anything about it, how come you didn't tell me?"

I fearfully replied, "I'm sorry, I forgot."

With all of her might and a mouth full of degrading words, she began to beat me in the top of my head. I guess she got tired of swinging with limited space, and realized that it wasn't causing as much pain outwardly as she would like to see.

So she stopped swinging, and just pulled my hair as hard as she possibly could for a long time, attempting to pull it out. Although only a small portion of hair actually came out, the pain was severe!

Excruciating!

I still have a very sore and tender spot in the top of my head from the many times that she beat me in the same spot, and pulled my hair.

Samantha: Oh God! What happened when this was over?

Layla: She said, "Get Out!"

So I got out of the car, and went back into the house- hurt physically and emotionally. I was embarrassed, and desperately wanted someone to help me. I fearfully laid on the couch, and went to sleep.

Interview Paused.

Chapter Three

ENOUGH

*T*he drugs and alcohol was taking over her mother's life. She wanted it, and she didn't care who was affected by it.

Some days their home was the drug lab. Pyrex glass containers, and wire hangers were among the ingredients, and a strong foul smell from the kitchen would fill every room of the house, wall to wall. No matter where Layla went or what she did, there was no escaping the smell, unless she went outside.

Her mother had no problem with doing drugs in Layla's face. She and her friends would be so high that Layla would see grown men crawling around on the floor like animals, saying weird things, and looking at Layla like they were ready to attack any second.

Layla and her older brother were left alone at home, sometimes for days without any adult supervision-forced to fend for themselves. If not at home alone, they were often dropped off with just about anyone that her mother thought was her friend.

She felt guilty about leaving them Layla with other people sometimes, but that didn't stop her from doing what she wanted to do. She would just go to the club where she hung out most of the time, and indulge in lots of drinks, dancing, and partying; while Layla and her brother sat in the car-sometimes for five or six hours at night by themselves.

Anger and hostility oozed from her mother's pores. She seemed to always be upset- until of course, she reached a certain high. She was angry if she wasn't high, and she was angry if she wasn't high enough. Miraculously, she would somehow transform when she had reached an ultimate high, and couldn't get any higher. It was then that she mellowed out, and was calm.

There were times when she called Layla by her actual name, but most of the time, she called her everything but Layla.

Think about it, could you imagine the amount of pain that's inflicted when a young girl's mother calls her profane names? Any cuss word that comes to your mind, Layla's mother most likely called her that. She would also say,

"You make me sick!"

When nine in a half times out of ten, Layla was wondering,

"What did I even do?"

Usually, it was something that didn't amount to much; like, not giving her mother a message if someone called, or not completing a chore to her mother's expectation.

Those are reasons to be disciplined or corrected, but certainly not something to be cussed out or given a black eye for. Layla's mother could barely hold a conversation without cussing and fussing.

It was hurtful.

It was confusing.

It was degrading.

Layla did whatever she could to make things better, but it never really worked. She felt like her mother hated her deeply, and she wanted to get away from her. She wanted to live with somebody-anybody, but her mother.

Spitefully, her mother never wanted to release custody of her. She didn't want to be exposed. She didn't want everyone else to know that there were real problems going on in their home. Or better yet, she didn't want to admit it to herself. Layla and her brother were forced to live through it. They were her crutch, some of her most used possessions.

She cussed them out anywhere, and in the presence of anybody. They could be in the grocery store, a restaurant, a hospital, it just didn't matter. At times people-often strangers; would try to intervene and help, but she would cuss them out to. It was so embarrassing! People were afraid of her.

Layla was totally amazed by the number of adults who seemed to be afraid of her mother, and could do no more than feel sorry for her and her brother.

Being called a plethora of hateful names very often; eventually became a part of Layla's own thoughts. After a while, those labels began to get in her head, and make her believe that everything her mother said was true-it was all her fault. Everything that ever happened was because of something that Layla did wrong. The devil was playing with Layla's mind daily. He was planting seeds in Layla that soon grew into gigantic trees of deception.

Layla's mother would hatefully say that she was crazy and weird because she enjoyed being alone, and she didn't get involved in much of anything.

She called Layla names that sent love out of the window and Layla's self-esteem in a one hundred mile per hour downward spiral. She called her every name that a person might want to call their worst enemy, but certainly not their daughter. Layla was a nervous mess. She would bite her nails down to the skin until they bled, and then she would gnaw her way up along the side of her fingers until they were sore.

This undoubtedly led to Layla becoming an introvert. She didn't participate in the things that "normal" children participated in all the time. Layla was a loner, and it was for good reason.

Thankfully, she knew that writing about what she was going through and how she felt would give her temporary relief. So that's what she did. She enjoyed writing poems, songs, and plays in the comfort of her room, all alone with the door closed.

Whenever Layla's mom felt that she had done something worthy of a whipping-which never was actual whippings, she would immediately start cussing her out. Calling her low down, hateful names and threatening to kill her. Although Layla sometimes doubted that her mother would actually do that, she knew that there was a definite possibility that she might. She knew that her mother was out of her mind.

Below you will find a little more of the interview, which explains a few occasions in detail.

Samantha: Were there times when your mother was nice to you?

Layla: Only when she wanted something or she wanted to make it look like she really loved me, because she was trying to get something from someone. A lot of times, she used me to get what she wanted. Then I was her baby & her favorite. Many people had no clue what was going on, because she played it off real good.

Samantha: So, would you say that you were trapped?

Layla: Very much so! To the point that I wanted her dead! The verbal abuse was intense-flaming hot, and it caused me to deal with major mental issues. I began to get involved with a lot of unhealthy behaviors, and those things opened the door wider for the devil and his demons even more. Come to think of it, the enemy was setting me up.

Interview Paused.

Layla began to look back and think about what was going on in the spirit realm during that time.

Through research she found that demonic spirits had been deposited in, and transferred to her.

Demonic spirits are what we wrestle with daily. Ephesians 6:12 tell us that we wrestle not against flesh and blood, but against principalities, against powers, against the rulers of the darkness of this world, against spiritual wickedness in high places.

These evil and unclean spirits have no respect of persons. They will come in to the smallest of children, and the oldest of adults; causing individuals to work for Satan.

It's important to walk with God and do exactly as scripture says in order to close every door that has ever been opened to the enemy, and keep them closed.

The doors here are referring to a person's five senses: see, touch, taste, hear, and smell. A person must be extremely careful how they operate and handle these senses, because they are the doors that the enemy uses to come in.

The devil loves to target really young children, because most often they have not been taught how the enemy works.

For those children that are being taught, but haven't yet gotten enough spiritual strength to war against the devil; the parents are held to a very high standard, and must war for them. It's of the utmost importance that parents are in a right relationship with God, and possess the power to battle for their children.

> **Author's Note:** **Please know; if there is a door open, evil spirits will enter in, and they will do everything they can to take control of an individual. The spirit realm is more real than the natural realm. However, most people only care to know about the natural realm. They refuse to dig deeper to understand how God and his angels work on our behalf; all while Satan and his angels form strategic plans against us.**
>
> **Hosea 4:6 says; it's because of the lack of knowledge that people are destroyed.**

Satan is constantly seeking who he can devour. His mission is for people to serve him and not God, because then he is adding to his kingdom. Everything that God has and does; the devil tries to make his own version of it, causing so many people to be confused and out of the arc of God's safety.

If you're in the will of God, It's nothing to be afraid of, however it's most definitely something to be educated and prepared for. Just as sure as we have night and day, the enemy is on the prowl, lurking for our souls.

So again, the abuse opened the door for a plethora of demonic spirits to be deposited in Layla. Although she was not outwardly violent, she definitely wrestled with violent thoughts very often. So much hatred was packed in her heart for her mother, and everyone else around her that knew what was going on and could help, but wouldn't.

Chapter Four
CRUSHED

*T*here were a number of different men in and out of their home. Layla was made to call those men Uncle, Mister, or even Daddy at times. She probably had about seven or eight supposed-to-be daddies in her lifetime.

She was forced to call those men dad and accept them as dad. However, it didn't take long for her to realize that none of those men were her dad. Layla's mother used her to get what she wanted from them. Often times, money and drugs.

There were times that her mother brought men home with her late at night. They were invited into Layla's room and left alone!

Young boys that Layla dated were encouraged to come over and stay the night, many times against

Layla's wishes. They were encouraged to stay in her room, although her mother knew that she would not be home to supervise. It was as if she wanted something to happen to Layla, like she wanted her to do things that would ruin her life.

Boom! Boom! Boom! Boom! Boom!

"Layla!"

Boom! Boom! Boom! Boom! Boom!

"Layla!"

Boom! Boom! Boom! Boom! Boom!

Layla rolled out of bed to see what all the noise was about. She could hear banging on the front door, and banging on her bedroom window. She then heard her mother yelling her name.

Layla tried peeking out of the window, but she couldn't see clearly; the window was very foggy. Super nervous and afraid, she had no idea what to expect when she went to the door. Out of habit, Layla asked,

"Who is it?"

Her mother replied,

"It's yo Momma, open the doe!"

Layla could tell by the sound of her mother's voice that she was fully loaded- super drunk, and under the influence of something. After all, it was around three o'clock in the morning, and she hadn't seen her mother in about twenty four hours.

Layla went to bed not expecting to be frightfully awakened by her mother beating on the window.

She opened the door, and could see her mother standing there with a man. She quickly turned around, and went back to her room. She closed the door, turned the light off, and got back in the bed. She was attempting to forget about what had just happened; and go back to sleep. Her Mother opened the door. Layla thought,

"I just wanna go to sleep, what could she want now?" Layla just laid there, and didn't say a word.

Her mother turned on the light, came in the room, stood around for a second or two; then she said,

"I brought someone to see you."

Layla was wondering what she was talking about. She looked up at her, and the two of them locked eyes. Layla could see the gloss on her mother's eye balls from all of the alcohol that she had consumed, but she wasn't quite sure what the look that her mother had just given her really meant.

The man that came home with her mother stepped into Layla's room. Layla was still in the bed, and she had the blanket pulled over her. She just looked at him. The man came all the way in the room, and sat on the side of the bed. Layla watched as her mother walked out of the room, closed the door, and then said,

"I'm gone leave ya'll alone!"

Fearful, Layla slowly slid up towards the head of the bed until she was touching the head board.

Still fully covered with the blanket, the man turned and looked at Layla. He began to ask her questions,

"How have you been doing?" he asked.

Layla mumbled, "Good."

He then said, "I haven't seen you in a long time." Layla didn't say anything, she just laid there quietly!

The man then comfortably leaned back and placed one of his arms across Layla's lap. At that point, Layla's heart began to race. The man leaned in closer, and looked Layla directly in the eyes. Layla began to breathe and blink really fast, and really hard. She knew that this was not about to be good.

The man began to kiss Layla on her lips. The strong smell of alcohol on his breath made Layla gag. She tightened her lips, and began to try and wiggle her way out of the situation. The man became more aggressive, and began to force his tongue in Layla's mouth.

"Momma!"

"Momma!"

"Momma!" Layla screamed!

She desperately wanted, and needed her mother's help. However, her mother shockingly responded with,

"I'm not coming in there!"

The man was still on Layla using his weight to restrain her, while Layla was screaming, and doing all she could to wiggle her way out.

Again, she screamed and yelled for her mother to help.

"Momma!"

"Momma!"

"Momma!"

"I need you!"

Her mother responded,

"I'm not coming to help you! That's ya'll business."

Layla just laid there. She was so amazed and heartbroken by her mother's response. She stopped fighting, wiggling, and yelling. In that moment, what the he was doing to her, felt like nothing compared to the pain of her mother's piercing remarks.

"Why won't she come and help me?" Layla thought angrily!

In Layla's mind, that was it. She had come to

the final conclusion that her mother hated her, and wanted to destroy her. Layla felt betrayed and alone.

Eventually, the man noticed that Layla was laying there lifeless. He pulled himself off of her, stood there and gathered himself, then walked out of the room. He left the light on, but closed the door.

Layla was furious! She thought.

"How could she?"

"What did she mean by, I'm not coming to help you?"

"What kind of mother does this to her daughter?"

Layla was thankful that the man stopped and left the room when he did; but she was so angry with her mother.

Sexual abuse had become normal to Layla. By the time this happened, she was almost a teenager and had already suffered a number of sexual abuse episodes that involved both men and women. This time was different though. Her mother was there, and she knew what was happening, but she refused to help.

The sexual abuse began before Layla was five years old. Many people knew that Layla didn't have any "protection" at home, so she became easy prey.

Her mother would leave her and her brother with friends, neighbors, relatives, or even by themselves at home for days at a time. They were on their own; eating whatever was available, and fending for themselves. Although it was rough to be alone, or left at just anybody's house regularly; anything and any place seemed to be better than being with their mother.

They were afraid to tell anyone what was going on because they knew that it would only make things worse. Their mother was very adamant about keeping home business at home. She threatened them every time they went anywhere that she thought questions would be asked. She would say,

"If they ask you anything, tell them to ask yo Momma!"

And so, they were forced to keep quiet most of the time.

Layla and her oldest brother were the only children their mother had for a while, but after they were a little older, their mother decided to start having more children. She had another son first, and then another daughter. Layla loved them very much. She babysat and took care of them a lot. She couldn't protect them from everything, but she certainly tried.

One day while at a baby sitters house, Layla and her younger brother were in a back room watching television alone. The baby sitter spent much of the day sitting on the couch watching television, talking on the phone, and watching what was going on outside. Her focus and attention was not on what was going on inside of her home, as much as what was going on outside of her home. She had an adult son staying with her, and he was in a separate room in the back of the house as well.

Knowing that his mother would not be coming to the back of the house anytime soon, he crept his way into the bedroom where Layla and her little brother were. He presented himself very friendly.

"What you watching?" He asked.

"Cartoons," Layla replied

He appeared to really enjoy watching cartoons himself. As he talked, he inched closer to the bed where the two children were sitting, and then laid across the top of the bed. He didn't make a move suddenly, but he waited for a little while; just long enough to make Layla feel comfortable with him being there. Once he talked to Layla and made her laugh long enough, he started to make his move on her.

He began to touch Layla, but she did not make a sound. This kind of thing happened so often, that it seemed like something that was supposed to happen. She turned her head towards her brother. As he sat there starring at her, she was hoping that he was too young to realize what was going on.

All she could think in her mind was, "My baby brother is sitting right there!"

Layla was concerned about her brother. She knew what was happening was wrong, but based on previous experiences; she felt that it would not do any good to say anything. She only wanted it to hurry and be over.

The door remained opened the entire time this was going on. You could hear the sound of the television, and the baby sitter talking on the phone. She never went to the back of the house to check on the children. This man knew what he was doing. He left the door opened so that if his mother did get up, he would be able to hear her coming. Once he was done and had been satisfied, he got up, fixed his clothes, and walked out of the room.

What happened in that room was something that Layla would always remember; something that would replay in her mind continuously for days, weeks, months, even years!

After he left, Layla took a deep breath, then got up and went into the bathroom to clean off. While she was in the bathroom, she could hear him walk through the house as if nothing had happened. He disappeared into his room, and didn't come back out for a while.

Layla went into the living room where the baby sitter was, everything in her wanted to tell what happened; but once again fear gripped Layla's heart, mind, and tongue. She could hardly speak. She walked through the living room, and as usual, saw the babysitter talking on the phone. She stood and looked out the door, and then went back to the room where her brother was. She laid across the bed and went to sleep until it was time to go home.

The baby sitter never knew what happened that day. Layla learned a little while later about the same man previously spending time in prison for child molestation. He hadn't been released too long before the encounter with her.

Layla wondered, "If she knew that, why would she allow him to be around me?"

Once again, she found herself crushed, and feeling like there was no one to talk to. So she just kept going, and kept everything bottled inside.

As a result of the abuse, Layla struggled with bed wetting for many years. It was shameful. She would do all that she could to not wet the bed, but it almost always happened. People around her didn't understand what was going on in her mind, or the way that she often felt.

She was talked about, laughed at, and picked on about it. Whenever she wet the bed at home, her mother would be so upset. She feared what would happen if her mother found out. So, she often tried her best to hide it from her.

One day her mother had gotten fed up with the bed wetting, and she went off! She started cussing Layla out, and threatening to make her sleep in the bath tub. Layla knew that her mother was crazy, but she didn't think that she would really make her spend the night in a cold bath tub.

"Come on, Get in here!" her Mother said.

What Layla feared was actually happening. Her mother was making her sleep in the bath tub. Layla's heart was pounding as she stepped over into the cold bath tub and laid down. Her mother walked out of the bathroom and closed the door.

Layla looked all around her and couldn't believe where she was. The sound of the dogs barking, and the cars driving by outside were so loud. She looked up at the window and could see the dark, starry sky through the cracks in the blinds. Again she felt so hurt and alone. She closed her eyes, and eventually went to sleep.

Scccch!

The sound of the shower curtain being pulled back startled Layla! She jumped and looked up to see her mother standing there.

"How did it feel sleeping in the bath tub?" her Mother said.

Layla just looked away, and didn't say a word. Her mother then said,

"Bet ya didn't pee on yoself in there did you?" "No", Layla replied.

Her mother said, "Get up!"

Layla stood up, stepped out of the tub, and went to her room.

Bed wetting was a problem, but it wasn't Layla's only issue. After being sexually abused by both men and women, Layla became very promiscuous and engaged in sexual activities with a number of people-just about anywhere. Her sex drive was at a level that she didn't know how to handle. It was totally out of control. For a while, Layla thought unless actual intercourse was taking place, it wasn't sex. However, she later learned about the different types of sexual activity. Before she was fourteen years old, she had been a partaker of just about every kind.

Things had gotten to the point where if someone approached her in a sexual way, she didn't turn it down. This included people that she knew very well, as well as people that she barely knew; and it involved both male and female. There were a ton of her peers involved in the same kind of sexual behavior, and their parents had no clue.

Often times, this behavior was displayed during sleep overs, and would be initiated by what seemed to be a harmless gesture on either person's part. Tickling and or wrestling with one another was common. Laughter filled the atmosphere, but all along, their hands were venturing in places that they had no business venturing to; and within a few minutes they were engaged in full blown sexual pleasure.

This happened in public places as well; in the park, on the back of a bus, and in the back seat of a car-to name a few. Layla was addicted to the pleasure of sex. So much so, that when she wasn't able to receive such pleasure with another person, she would use objects; pillows, stuffed animals, or whatever she could use to get the pleasure that she felt she needed.

Layla was deeply in a bad place. She was struggling, fighting, and suffocating inside. She didn't want to be where she was. She didn't want to do what she was doing, but she didn't know how to not do it. It was a part of who she was, or at least that's what she thought.

Chapter Five
CALL HIM DADDY

ing, Ring, Ring!
Ring, Ring, Ring!
The phone was ringing. Layla rushed to answer it. She knew that her mother would have a fit if it rang too many times.

Layla said, "Hello."

"What are ya'll doing that you couldn't answer the phone?" Her mother said.

"I was trying to get to it as fast as I could." Layla responded

"Yea, well I'm on my way home."

"I'm bringing someone with me that wants to see you." Her mother explained.

Layla said, "Ok."

She was about to hang up the phone when her mother quickly said, "Call him Daddy."

Layla was a bit confused, but said "Ok."

She hung the phone up, and began to wonder what her mother was talking about. She could tell by the sound of her voice that she had been drinking, so she didn't know what to expect.

Her mother arrived at the house. She came through the door, and then a man followed her shortly after. Her mother was loud; and very smart mouthed toward him, but she was being very nice to Layla.

The man came in and just looked with a blank stare. It was as if he was stuck. He watched Layla, but he didn't say much to her.

Her mother said,

"Yea, she's yours."

"She looks just like you."

He still didn't say much to Layla, but he soon began talking to her mother.

A few minutes later, Layla's mother told her to stand next to him and take a picture. Layla did as she was told, and then she walked to the back of the house.

She was going to her grandfather's house that evening, so she just waited until it was time to go.

About an hour had passed when her mother said, "Ok, let's go!"

They hoped up into that man's big truck, and he drove them to her grandfather's house on the other side of town.

When they arrived, her mother got out of the truck and went inside the house. She left Layla in the truck with the man.

He said to her mother, "What are you doing?"

She responded, "You can get her."

He looked back at Layla, then he got out of the truck and walked around to the side where Layla was sitting.

Very nicely he said, "Come on, you wanna get down?"

Layla stood up, and he helped her down. Layla noticed how nice he was.

She was curious about him being so nice, and wondered who he really was; so she asked,

"Are you a friend of my Dad?"

He said, "What?"

"Your mother didn't tell you who I am?"

Layla responded, "No."

He said, "Well, we gone have to ask her about that."

Then the two of them walked in the house

together. Layla noticed that he didn't say anything to her mother right away about it, they just went on.

Layla didn't say anything, but it was in the back of her mind. The next day that same man came to visit again. Her mother welcomed him inside, and then looked at Layla and said,

"This is your daddy."

Layla didn't know what to think. She was confused. She couldn't help but think about all of the other men that her mother said was her daddy.

She didn't question it though. She just looked at him, said hello, and then walked to her room

Her dad came around a lot, and he made sure that she had what she needed. He even got her some of the things she wanted. It took Layla a while but she was starting to like having him around. She was starting to feel like everything was going to be alright.

A few days later, her dad came by and he brought another little girl with him.

"This is your sister," he said.

Layla looked at her, smiled slightly, and said, "Hi."

She was about three years younger than Layla, and they didn't seem to like each other much in the beginning. They were trying to understand all of what was going on.

Layla's dad had a family when he met her, but that didn't stop him from coming around and looking after her when he could.

Her sister's mom didn't like for him to be at their house. She would come over late at night-upset, fussing, and cussing; threatening her dad's life.

But he still kept coming. Things were feeling right to Layla. She didn't show it much, but she was excited to finally get to know that man that she had always wanted to meet; her dad.

He was with her one day, and then gone the next day. It was like he just disappeared. She didn't see or talk to him or her sister anymore. It hurt Layla immensely! She was just getting used to having them around.

She went on though, and after a while, she just tried to pretend that she never met them in the first place.

Chapter Six

I CAN'T BREATHE

"*L*ayla what's wrong?"

"Are you ok?"

That was the sound of her grandmother's voice when she walked into the bathroom and found Layla fighting for her life.

Layla was diagnosed with asthma as a baby, and had always struggled to keep her breathing under control. One cool, fall evening Layla was having trouble breathing. She hadn't been feeling good all day, but never told anyone. She figured that she would be ok. "It's no different than any other time," she thought.

She had auditioned for the school talent show, and made the cut to perform. Her grandmother picked her up after school, and took her shopping to pick out a dress. As they walked through the malls, in and out of each store; and then in and out of the cool air outside, Layla could feel her chest getting tighter and tighter.

Her grandmother noticed that she seemed like something was wrong,

"You feel alright?" she asked.

"I've just been wheezing all day, I'll be alright though." Layla said.

"Where is your inhaler?" her grandma asked.

"I left it at home." Layla replied.

Her grandmother looked at her with much concern, but Layla did her best to pretend as if she was ok. She was excited to go shopping for the dress that she would wear in the talent show. Time was moving along, and she didn't want to wait any longer.

They went to one mall and didn't find much, so they picked out a maybe dress. After that, they decided to stop by another mall for one last look on their way to her great grandmother's house. They arrived at the mall; got out of the car and walked in, but Layla was struggling. Yet she still kept going as if nothing was wrong. Thankfully, they were able to find a dress rather quickly, but it was way too long for Layla. Her grandmother said,

"Well, if that's the one that you want, we'll take

it over to Granny and have her pin the bottom, then take it to be hemmed for you."

Layla was excited! She liked that idea, so she said, "Ok, this is the one that I want!"

They bought the dress, got back in the car, and then drove to her great grandmother's house. Layla's grandmothers were smokers. There were thick clouds of cigarette smoke that seemed to fill every corner of the house that evening. Her grandmother said,

"Go put the dress on so that it can be pinned." Layla went into the restroom; changed clothes, then came back out. When she came out of the restroom, her grandmother told her exactly where and how to stand.

She said, "Stand over there, stand up straight, and be still."

Layla did as she was told to the best of her ability; however she was struggling to be still. She felt as if she was going to fall. She kept moving, and it was frustrating her grandmothers to no end. They kept saying,

"Layla, be still!" but Layla couldn't.

She replied, "I'm trying, but I can't!"

The strong smell of smoke, and Layla already having trouble breathing; was not mixing well at all. Eventually, Layla's great grandmother was fed up.

She said, "Just go take the dress off, I don't know what's going on with you!"

Layla walked over to the restroom- that was only a few steps away, she went in, closed the door, and locked it. Her heart was racing. Something was happening that she could not explain or control. She was experiencing such excruciating pain that she couldn't take the dress off. The pain in her stomach felt as if someone was stabbing her repeatedly, and she was consumed with an overwhelming feeling of not being able to breathe.

She folded over on the sink in desperation for air and relief. She could feel the pain extending from her stomach to every portion of her body; suddenly crippling her. Her body was shutting down. Her grandmother knocked on the door, and asked again,

"Are you ok?"

Layla could hardly speak, she mumbled, "No."

"Unlock the door!" her grandmother replied! Still folded over the sink, Layla extended her arm to the door and unlocked it. Her grandmother opened the door.

"Layla, what's wrong?" she said.

"I can't breathe, and my body hurts badly!" said Layla.

Her grandmother said "ok, go ahead and get dressed." She turned around and walked to the phone. She called Layla's mother, and Layla could hear her talking on the phone.

She said, "Get Layla's breathing machine ready, we are on our way!"

Layla managed to get dressed; then she walked out of the bathroom. Her grandmother was gathering her things so that they could leave. Layla decided to wait outside because she felt like she needed some fresh air. As she waited outside, she felt zoned- out of it.

Her grandmother went outside; they got in the car, and began to drive away. As they drove down the street, Layla began to feel worse. All of a sudden she could no longer see. Her eyes were open, but everything was black. She remained calm, but she was afraid of what was happening. She started asking her grandmother questions. She felt like if she just sat there, she was going to die. Her grandmother answered a few questions, but soon told Layla to stop talking, and save her breath. Layla was obedient and just sat there quietly.

Thankfully, they didn't have to drive far to get

to Layla's house. They pulled up at the house and her grandmother said,

"Sit here, while I go get someone to help you out of the car."

She got out and walked in the house. Layla felt horrible! She felt as if she was taking her final breath. Panicking, she got out of the car and stumbled around to the front yard. She made it almost to the porch before she collapsed. She fell on her face in the front yard, lifeless. She was not breathing at all. She lost her bowels and every blood vessel in her eyes busted due to the lack of oxygen to her brain.

Her older brother and a young man, who was always like a big brother to her, came out and lifted her off of the ground. The ambulance arrived shortly after that. They put her on the stretcher, and attempted to do C.P.R., but it didn't work. She was still lying there, lifeless. They cut her clothes off and pulled out the defibrillator. After a few minutes of using the device, Layla began to breathe again.

Although breathing, she still laid there lifeless. Many test and procedures were performed on Layla once she arrived to the hospital, but nothing seemed to give the answers that the doctor's needed.

Layla had gone into a coma, and was not able

to see, feel, or hear anything for days. After about four days, Layla opened her eyes and saw people standing at the foot of her bed. They could not tell that her eyes had opened, and Layla was not able to talk. Soon after, a lady walked in the room. She was wearing a red suit, and she had an arm full of papers. She walked over to the side of the bed where Layla was laying and began to talk.

She said, "Hi Layla, my name is Jennifer Smith and I am a social worker here at the hospital.

How are you feeling?"

Not sure if she could talk, Layla opened her mouth and said,

"What happened?"

Jennifer replied, "You passed out, and you've been out of it for a few days.

Is it ok if I ask you some questions?"

Layla nodded her head, yes.

Jennifer began asking Layla questions about home. She asked about her mother and if she was treating her right. Out of fear, Layla replied, yes. She convinced Jennifer that everything was ok at home. Once Jennifer was done asking questions she left the room. Layla laid there trying to process everything that was going on. Doctor after doctor entered the room; they were amazed at the sight of Layla sitting up in the bed, talking, and requesting food. They never had a full explanation for what happened to Layla, but because she seemed to be doing alright, they were willing to release her to go home.

The next day Layla was released, and her mother went to pick her up. When she arrived, she had been drinking and was on full. She seemed happy to see Layla, but was very smart mouthed and impatient with the hospital staff. She rolled Layla out of the room in a wheel chair, and took her to the car.

They made it home, but life was far from normal for Layla! Her eyes were crimson red from the blood vessels that busted. She was afraid to look at herself in the mirror. It was like something from a horror movie. She had numerous doctor appointments and tests. Having to wear a pace maker to monitor her heart, and oxygen tubes in her nose to help her breathe, made it difficult to attend school. She was home for a while before she could return.

Classmates would come by to visit and be terrified by the sight of Layla. Her eyes alone were scary. Many of them would stop at the door and refuse to go any further. Layla tried welcoming them inside, but they often replied,

"I just can't stand to see you that way." Although

Layla understood, and was in full agreement that she looked scary; she became discouraged and sad when others didn't want to be around her. During this time, she wasn't allowed to go far but when she just needed some fresh air, she would sit on the front porch. People passing by would just stare. She understood that her eyes caught their attention, but she didn't let it bother her too much. She just took a deep breath and continued to enjoy the fresh air.

Not long after Layla recovered, and was able to return to normal daily activities, things were again pretty rough at home. Her mother continued to be abusive, and Layla just wanted to get away from it all. She began staying with different people for extended periods of time; some she barely knew, just so she wouldn't have to deal with the pressure and stress of being at home.

Layla began staying with a family that had always been fairly close to her family. It was a number of people that lived there before Layla came, but she didn't care. She just didn't want to go home. So everyone made room for her, they all made it work. They were all like family. There were times that they argued, didn't get along, were very frustrated and irritated just like any other family, but Layla appreciated them so much for allowing her to come and stay.

This particular family was one that attended church regularly. Everyone in the house didn't always go but Gigi, the mother and grandmother of the house, would go faithfully; along with most of the children. Layla always found a reason to not go to church with them whenever they went.

One weekend the church was taking a trip to a nearby amusement park.

"Layla, our church is going to Kings Island; would you like to go with us?

Layla wasn't sure how she would pay for it, but she did want to go. She called and asked her grandmother for the money to go on the trip. Her grandmother said "Yes", and soon met Layla in front of the house to give her the money.

Layla was super excited, but yet a little nervous. She didn't know what to expect, or how things would go, but she was looking forward to having fun. While they were on the trip, Layla enjoyed herself thoroughly.

In the midst of having fun, she found herself watching the people from the church who were around her, and she was taking serious mental note. She watched how they walked, how they talked, and how they responded to one another.

She was impressed! So much so, that she decided to go to church with them sometimes.

She started going to church soon after that, and to her surprise, she enjoyed being there. She enjoyed being in a place where she felt loved and wanted, that alone meant so much to her at the time. The people there praised, and danced, and sang so wonderfully. Then the Pastor would preach so powerfully, exhausting everything in him. He seemed to always know just what to say. Layla couldn't comprehend a lot of what he was saying, but she enjoyed hearing him.

Layla didn't know the scriptures, or the books of the Bible, or who the people were from the Bible that he mentioned in his messages, but she sat and pretended to know. She tried with everything in her to understand.

One summer, on a Sunday afternoon, they were in the midst of a great time at church, and the Pastor had preached a powerful message as usual. When he was finished preaching, he extended an opportunity for someone to be saved. The church always called it -opening the doors of the church. The pastor talked for what seemed like a really long time, and Layla didn't really understand a thing that he was saying; besides "Come, would you come?" After he said, "Come" a number of times, Layla tuned in. She began to feel as if he was talking directly to her. She soon felt a strong urge to get up and go sit in the chair.

Nervous and somewhat afraid, she looked around at the other people there. She caught the attention of Gigi who was sitting in the choir stand, and they locked eyes for a brief moment. Gigi could tell that Layla was battling and trying to decide if she should go or not. Without saying a word, Gigi simply nodded her head forward, as if to say "It's ok", and Layla stood up and walked, lighter than ever, to the front of the church, and sat in the chair. Once Layla really realized where she was, she began to think, "What am I doing? Why am I up here?" It felt as if someone or something lifted her out of her seat, and walked her to the front of the church; although no one in the room had touched her.

Again, Layla was very nervous; but what was happening felt so right. That was the day that Layla asked God to forgive her sins, and she received Jesus Christ as her Lord and Savior. She didn't know a whole lot, but she learned as she went. The more she went, the more she learned, and the more she grew. She eventually got involved with a number of activities and auxiliaries around the church that kept her busy.

Layla stayed close to the older people, because they seemed to have what she wanted and needed. She wanted to know how to do the things that they did. The church taught her so much about life, but more importantly about God.

Chapter Seven
"HE'LL BE BACK"

ayla attended church on Friday evenings. One specific Friday, she went by her mom's house to visit before she went to church. She sat at the table and talked to her mom as she moved about in the house doing other things. Her mother stopped for a second and asked, "When was the last time that you talked to your brother?"

Layla replied, "I don't know."

Her mother picked up the phone and dialed his number, then passed the phone to Layla so they could talk. Layla and her brother talked for a few minutes, and before they ended the conversation he promised that he would come by and see her before she left.

He said, "I need to make a stop and then I'll be there."

Layla said "ok, looking forward to seeing you."

They both said "bye," and hung up the phone.

Seconds later the phone rang again, and it was her brother calling back. Layla was thinking that he simply forgot to say something, she answered the phone.

"Hello!" Layla said.

"Layla, where's Momma?" Her brother asked in a calm but urgent voice.

"In the back, you want to talk to her?" Layla asked.

"Yes," He replied.

Layla called for her mother to come to the phone.

"Hello!" Her mother said.

"What? What's wrong? Where are you at?" She yelled!

She laid her forehead on the wall, and began to bang her fist.

Her mother shouted, "No, No, No, I'm on my way!"

She threw the phone down, put on her snow suit-that she wore all the time, and ran out of the back door. Layla was left there with her new baby sister, and she didn't know what was going on. She had someone coming to pick her up for church soon, but wasn't sure what to do.

Not long after, a friend of the family- that came around often; stopped by and said that he would stay with her baby sister. Layla's ride was waiting outside, so she got in the car and went to church. When the service was over Layla and some of the other church members were sitting around talking for a while. As Layla was walking out of the door getting ready to go home, she could hear the phone at the church ring, but she didn't think much about it. She continued walking and was almost in the car when she heard someone yelling her name. She stopped and looked to see who it was. It was her Pastor's wife. Layla walked back across the street where she was standing. The two of them looked at each other and she said to Layla, "I'm sorry, your brother was just killed." Devastated and unsure what to do, Layla began pacing the sidewalk. Her thoughts were racing.

"How could this be? This can't be true? What do I do? Is this real? I just talked to him earlier today!" Eventually the ladies that were standing out there grabbed Layla and hugged her for a while, before they helped her to the car.

They drove her to her grandmother's house. When they arrived, no one was there, but Layla had a key. She opened the door and went inside; she was still not sure how to deal with it, so she just sat at the table. The ladies came in and sat with her until someone else came. It seemed as if no one ever thought to find Layla so that she could be at the hospital with the rest of the family.

After sitting there for a while waiting to hear from someone, her grandmother walked through the door, and confirmed that it was true. Her brother had been murdered. He was shot in the head. Heartbroken, Layla walked to the back of the house to her brother's room, and laid across his bed. She didn't realize that she was still there until early the next morning when her grandmother woke her up and told her to get dressed.

Layla was still devastated and in shock, none of it seemed to be real. It all felt like a dream that Layla was having.

"He's just on vacation for a while!"

"He'll be back!" Layla thought.

Seeing that Layla had recently accepted Jesus as her Lord and Savior just a couple of months before this happened; she seemed to be dealing with it well- perhaps a little too well for some of her relatives. They were expecting her to show some kind of outward emotion, but it was as if she couldn't. Yes, her eyes filled with tears at times, and her heart was hurt; but something was keeping the tears from falling uncontrollably. Something was keeping her sane. Something was holding her up. Something was giving her peace when everyone else was distraught.

She later found out that she was experiencing the peace of God. She had a peace that could not be explained, and although she wanted to break down, she simply couldn't.

This made so many of her relatives upset, suspicious, and lead to think that she didn't care. It wasn't that at all. God was just holding her up in a marvelous way.

None of it seemed real to Layla until ten years later, when she went by his grave site with a group of family members. Not thinking that she would be affected much by the visit, she got out of the car and walked to the tombstone. She looked down and saw his picture, and then the tears began to roll uncontrollably. She had finally come to grips. She thought to herself,

"He's actually gone and he's not coming back."

Chapter Eight

COME ON, LET HER GO

*A*fter her brother was murdered, Layla moved back home. She was hoping that things would be different. She was hoping that her mother didn't hate her anymore.

One Friday evening Layla was getting ready for church, but hadn't seen her mom in a day or so. She wasn't quite sure if she should leave home or not, but she thought,

"It's just church, I'll leave a note encase she comes home."

Layla wrote the note and left it on the refrigerator. While she was at church, her mother came home with a host of friends. They sat around smoking, and drinking.

Layla got in the car with her Pastor and his Wife after service, and they took her home. Knowing that she hadn't seen her mom in a while, she was pretty shocked to see lots of lights on, and cars parked in the yard when they arrived. She was fearful of what to expect when she walked in the house. She said goodnight to the Pastor, got out of the van, and walked up to the door.

There was a small window right next to the door that was completely broken out, and she could hear people talking as she unlocked the door. Her mother heard her coming in and met her. In a loud and angry voice she said,

"Where have you been? And who is that bringing you home?"

"I was at church, and that was the Pastor and his family bringing me home." Layla replied.

Her mother as usual began to call her names, and then yelled,

"When did it become ok for you to leave this house without asking me first?"

Confused by the question, and embarrassed because she knew that her Pastor and his family could hear what was going on, she said

"I left you a note".

"I ain't seen no note!" Her mother said.

"I left it on the refrigerator." Layla replied.

Her mother then began to go all in cussing her out. Layla couldn't tell if she was taking any breaths at all in between what she was saying. She was yelling so loud, and talking so fast, Layla could just feel that something was about to happen.

"Why would you leave a note for me on the refrigerator?

Just because all your fat self thinks about is eating?

Any other time, you would leave it on the table if you wanted me to see it.

What's so different about tonight?" Her mother said.

"I just thought that you would see it when you went into the kitchen." Layla answered.

Her mother went on to use more choice words, calling her names, and becoming more and more upset every second it seemed. Layla looked and noticed that all of her mother's guests were sitting at the table watching and listening to it all, while they continued to smoke and drink.

All of a sudden, it was as if a bomb exploded inside of her mother!

She reached forward, grabbed Layla by her hair, threw her to the ground, and started dragging her down the hall. She continued to call her all kind of names, while hitting her at the same time. Eventually, one of her mother's guests spoke up and said,

"Don't you think that's enough? Come on, let her go!"

That only made things worse. Her mother shifted her cuss out to the visitor, and then she said to him,

"Get out!"

Layla could hear the friend saying,

"Come on now! Where am I going to go? I rode with you!"

Her mother replied, "I don't care where you go, but you gotta get outta here!"

You ain't gone be in here trying to tell me how to raise my children!"

She turned and finished with Layla. Then she said,

"Don't go in your room, go in mine."

"And don't think you are going back to that church either!"

"I hope you enjoyed yourself tonight, because you won't be going back!"

Layla went to her mother's room. There wasn't much in there but a love seat, a dresser, a radio, and a few other things.

It felt cold and lifeless, just like her mother. Layla sat down on the couch, and covered up with a blanket that was lying nearby. Layla was so hurt; not only because of her mother beating her, but because she was going to keep her from church.

Layla was devastated!

She thought, "How could she?"

"What am I going to do?"

"Going to church is my only outlet."

Her mother locked her in the house, and demanded that she not leave to go anywhere. Layla put one of her favorite CD's in the radio, and set the speaker right next to her ear. She turned on one song, and set it to repeat. She listened to that song over, and over, and over again- all day and all night. The song, be encouraged, no matter what's going on, ministered to Layla as she laid on the love seat and cried every day.

A number of days had passed. She fearfully called one of her aunts while her mother was gone. Crying and upset, she expressed a lot of what was going on at home, and how she just wanted it to all be over.

Her aunt made the decision to try and help. She called CPS and filed a report. That afternoon, a lady from CPS arrived at their house. Thankfully,

Layla's mother was still gone. The lady knocked on the door. Layla went to the door and opened it slightly. The woman began asking questions, and trying to look in the house beyond Layla.

"May I come in?" she asked.

Layla feared that her mother might come home and see someone else in the house, so she replied, "I can't let you in."

I'm only here to help. You don't have to be afraid. The woman said.

Layla hesitantly said, "I can't."

The woman said, "If you don't let me in, I won't be able to help you very much. Layla was too afraid, and refused to let her in. So, the woman eventually left.

A few days later, Layla's mother received a letter in the mail. It demanded that she show up for a meeting with CPS. She and Layla went to the meeting, and were taken in two separate rooms for questioning. Layla was afraid, but excited. She was thinking,

"This is my way out!"

"I'm going to tell them what's been going on, and they're going to take me from her."

"Then everything will be better."

The CPS workers went back and forth from Layla's room to her mother's. After about an hour of questions, and writing things out for them to review, they came back in the room and said, "Alright, you're free to go!"

They released her back into the hands of her mother.

Layla thought,

"Oh No!"

"This can't be happening!"

"She's really going to kill me now!"

Her mind was going super-fast.

"How can this be?"

"What did she tell them?"

"How could they not believe me?" she thought.

She and her mother looked at each other, but neither of them said a word. They got on the elevator, and left the building. Once they got in the car, they both remained quiet for a moment, and then her mother began to go off.

"You got the nerve to have somebody report me to CPS?"

"When we get home you got work to do."

This time it wasn't as loud or as violent, because they were still in the parking lot.

Her mother was a bit afraid of what might happen with CPS, she didn't say much more after they returned home. Surprisingly, she just made Layla clean the house, and clean the house, and clean the house some more. After a few weeks, things smoothed over with C.P.S., and her mother was right back at it-fussing, cussing, and beating Layla as usual.

Chapter Nine

I JUST WANNA DIE

*E*ven after attending church for a while, Layla was still struggling mentally. Feelings of depression, rejection, and defeat filled Layla's heart and mind immeasurably!

She was so tired of living life and being hurt. No matter how hard she tried, it seemed as if she couldn't get a break. She couldn't understand why so many horrible things were happening to her, and nobody seemed to care.

The devil was deceiving Layla abundantly. She may not have had the people that mattered the most to her during that time, but God had provided so many others that stood in the gap.

Instead of looking at what God provided, she kept looking back to what she thought she needed.

One afternoon, Layla was at the church getting a few things done along with a few other church members. As they were finishing up, Layla just didn't feel good, she felt really down and really low. It was an unexplainable kind of feeling that she didn't quite understand. She knew that it was time to go home, but she was totally dreading it. She thought,

"I want to just stay at the church all day long, or go home with someone else."

She didn't mention anything to anyone because she was afraid of what they would think of her, or what they would do. She just waited for her ride home.

She got in the car and they began driving toward her house- which wasn't far from the church that she attended. She began to feel worse during the short drive. It was as if she was in some sort of zone. She pretended like everything was fine- smiling and talking as normal. She never mentioned how she was feeling.

They arrived at her house. She smiled and said, "Thank You for the ride."

"You're so welcome!" they happily replied.

She got out of the car, and fearfully walked in the house. She stood around for a little bit, and then walked into her bedroom. No one else was home, the house was very quiet.

She sat at the foot of the bed and just stared at different things. It was as if something else had taken possession of her entire body. She felt extremely heavy, sad, lonely, and afraid. Negative thoughts filled her mind to the max.

"What's the purpose for living? Nobody would care if I died."

"I would be better off anyway."

"At least I won't be here dealing with all of this pain anymore! It'll all be over." She thought.

Then she just sat there and continued to stare.

After a few minutes, more negative thoughts flooded her mind.

"Why did I ever have to wake up from the coma?"

"I wish I would have just stayed sleep forever."

"I'm only here to be hurt anyway."

The thoughts became stronger and stronger very quickly.

"It's time to die, I don't want to live anymore!" came to her mind.

But then, it was as if something else snatched her from that thought for a split second, and she could hear,

"No, it's not time to die! But, I do want to live."

She then heard, "Go ahead and kill yourself, you're here all alone. It's your perfect opportunity!"

"It can be all over right now, nobody's here to stop you."

But then she heard, "You don't want to do that." and she thought, "I can't do that."

"Yes you can!" rang louder in her ear. She began to give in and respond to the negative thoughts-dismissing all thoughts of wanting to live.

She got up and walked into the bathroom. She stood there and just stared at herself in the mirror for a few seconds.

She then thought, "How would I even do that?"

"I don't have a gun, and I'm not about to cut myself. So, that's not gone work."

She had gotten some dental work done shortly before that day, but didn't take all of the pain medicine that the doctor prescribed. It seemed to be too strong for her. The pill bottle was sitting in her room on the desk.

She thought, "I have those pills, I'll just take those. That should do the job."

She continued to look at herself and wonder if that was really something that she wanted to do. She didn't ponder long before she walked back to her bedroom, grabbed the pill bottle and looked at it.

She took the pills back to the bathroom, and again looked in the mirror. Her eyes went from the mirror to the pill bottle about three or four times before she actually opened the bottle. So afraid, but yet determined, she took about five pills and then just stood there waiting for something to happen; but nothing happened.

She quickly became very upset. She picked up the bottle and took all of the pills, except for three. Then she took the bottle back to her room. She wanted to leave some so that whoever found her wouldn't think that she actually killed herself with pills.

Nothing seemed to be happening at first, but after a few minutes she became very weak. Not knowing what was about to happen, she became really scared.

She thought, "No, I don't want to die!"

"Well, I do want to die that's why I did this."

"But No, I don't want to die!"

There was a war going on in her mind. She grabbed the phone, and with very little strength, she sat down on the floor next to the front door and called a close family friend for help.

"Hello." They answered.

Barely able to talk, Layla responded "Hi, are you busy?"

"Not really, what's up Layla?" They said.

"Can you come and get me?" Layla said.

"What's wrong?" They responded?

"I don't feel good. Will you take me to the hospital please?" Layla asked.

They initially thought that she was playing, and kind of laughed it off.

She said,

"I'm serious, I really don't feel good."

"Please come and get me!"

They responded, "We can call 911, they will be there faster! What's wrong?"

Layla begged, "No please don't call 911, just come and get me!"

Then totally depleted, Layla just laid on the floor. They arrived a short time later, and could see Layla laying there through the glass of the screen door. They began to call her name and bang on the door.

"Layla, unlock the door!" they shouted!

Layla looked up and was able to slowly reach her arm up to unlock the door, but was not able to stand.

They kept saying,

"Layla I'm calling 911!"

But, Layla just kept shaking her head and saying

"No, No!"

They picked her up and practically carried her to the truck. They kept talking to Layla, but Layla was very weak, and wasn't really responding. She was limp, and her speech was slurred. No matter how they asked Layla what happened, she simply would not say.

They continued to do all they could to keep Layla awake while they drove to the hospital. Layla kept hearing, "Stay with me, open your eyes, wake up, wake up, wake up!"

They arrived at the hospital and Layla was rushed into a room. Her entire body was numb, and she could hardly talk. The doctors ran every test that could be done, but couldn't find anything wrong. They kept going in and out of the room asking Layla questions, but no response.

Layla laid there, she was so upset and confused. "Why am I still here?"

"Why didn't it work?"

"I'm not supposed to be here!"

"No!" Layla thought.

All kind of different people entered the room, doctors, nurses, visitors, family members, and social workers. All of them asking questions, but not getting much response. The doctors were running out of tests, and didn't know what else to do.

So they called for a psychiatrist.

After much discussion amongst themselves, they decided that Layla was dealing with a mental health issue, and needed to be admitted to the psych. ward at the hospital.

Layla still laid there, she wasn't really sure what that meant, and she didn't care. She just wanted everything to be over. The doctors talked to the family and those that were gathered there with them. They explained the plan that they had decided.

Some of the family agreed, and some didn't.

They went back and forth with one another, trying to decide what to do. A friend of the family spoke up and said, "No she doesn't need to be there!" "She'll be fine!"

She turned and walked into the room where Layla was and began to talk to her.

She said, "Come on Layla, pull it together, you're going home!"

Curious, Layla looked at her and couldn't believe that she was actually going home. She thought,

"Why?"

"I can't be going home."

"I'm supposed to be dead."

"I don't want to go back home!"

But she never spoke that from her mouth. She just looked at her and listened to what she was saying.

Layla soon began to feel some parts of her numb body again, and was able to move. She stumbled out of bed and stood up. She walked over to her clothes and began to get dressed. The doctors agreed to release Layla, and wrote her a prescription for an anti-depressant.

Once Layla got home, she had so many mixed feelings. She cried a lot, wanted to be alone in the dark, and just couldn't understand why she wasn't dead.

The devil was doing all that he could to kill her. No matter what happened, or what didn't happen, God had His hand on Layla's life. It wasn't time for her to die. Layla was too young to understand, but God had a plan.

The Lord had already begun transforming Layla's life. She still battled with the hurt and pain from her past, but she was looking for a better way. She was looking for a better life than what she had always known and been taught.

The enemy was fighting hard. He was trying to totally destroy her. She had seen, and been involved with too much. He knew that if she ever really broke free; his kingdom would be in trouble.

Chapter Ten
GOD WILL PROVIDE!

*L*ayla felt safer being a part of the church and having others around to help her, but the long journey of deliverance and healing had only just begun.

She remained as faithful as possible to church, and she enjoyed every bit of it. However, when church was over she knew that she was going back home. Everything was different at home, and she never wanted to be there.

She desperately wanted to feel loved and understood. People often said, "I Love You," but it never meant much to Layla. She had a difficult time believing that they really meant it. She couldn't get past how many of them so often made her feel.

Layla didn't know how, and she didn't know

when it would happen, but she determined in her mind that the life she had known then; would not be her life always.

It was difficult for Layla at times, because no one else in her environment outside of church was saved, or even had a desire to attend church regularly.

Relatives and friends seemed to be okay with her attending church, but it was just too much that she really loved God with everything in her. They didn't understand that her heart's desire was to be set apart for God's use- nothing less. She was willing to trade everything that she was for all that God could make her to be.

Things were rough at church sometimes too. She loved being there, but it seemed that a number of people had a hard time understanding her. Some of them often made comments that made her feel like she was beneath them. She was expected to just fit in and catch on to things that they had always known and done.

They had not gone through what Layla had gone through. They had not been where Layla had been. It was a whole new world for her. She didn't know what they knew, and she hadn't been taught like they had been taught. She just kept watching and catching on, because she had a strong desire to know what they knew. She wanted to live the life that they lived. They seemed to be so free.

Layla stayed and learned; and eventually she began to see results. The pastor and his wife played a huge role in helping her to cultivate a love for Christ like never before.

The Lord began delivering Layla as a teenager, but the trauma from what she had gone through followed her into her adult life. So much of what she had been through was never dealt with, only swept from one rug to another. She didn't know how to totally break free.

For every season of Layla's life, God provided what she needed to make it through. He saw fit to bless Layla with amazing women of God who loved her, and only wanted the best for her. They were like her teachers and counselors in the spirit realm. They helped her to become stronger.

One evening, the Lord blessed Layla to hear a woman on television. It was a world renowned and powerful Christian woman, who often taught on prayer and having an intimate relationship with God. Layla was intrigued by her teachings, and began watching her faithfully. Before long, she began to put those things that she had been taught into practice. She began to feel and see her life changing completely.

<u>Author's Note:</u> Please hear me; if you are someone that God is using to impact the world, what you do always matters! You're the only hope that some people have. You are someone's way out or way through. For every person you may never meet; thank you for being obedient to God and allowing Him to use you.

A few years later, Layla was blessed once again and taken under the wings of a mighty woman of God that would become known as her spiritual mother. This woman loved Layla and her family, and she was there with them through the good, the bad, and the ugly. She never judged, but in love she taught, nurtured, and prayed. It meant the world to Layla to feel loved as a daughter, understood, and guided in the way of righteousness.

With the help of her spiritual mother and her pastor, she was on her way to total victory.

Chapter Eleven

LORD, SET ME FREE

O ver the years, Layla found ways to cope and make it from day to day. Most of the time she was able to push things aside and just keep moving; but in the back of her mind, she knew that one day she wouldn't be able to do that anymore.

She had finally come to the point where she was willing to go through the process of complete deliverance. A lot had already happened, but she yet had such a long way to go.

Layla knew that God was real; she could feel Him working mightily in her life. Deliverance had already taken place, but healing was needed. Without her noticing it; there were things that she was holding on to, and people that she had not forgiven. There were also people that she needed to apologize to in order for her to be totally free, and the ultimate healing process to begin.

Deliverance is something that a person must really want.

When a person surrenders, and their life is totally yielded to God; they become the perfect candidate for complete deliverance.

Deliverance from a place of bondage means that an individual is set free from the holding place that the devil once lured them to; and they have been made clean inside.

In order to stay clean, a person must quickly fill themselves with the things of God, and most importantly with the Word of God, until there is absolutely no room for the devil to operate in them.

Demonic spirits operate by going in and fastening themselves to an individual, causing them to be bound, and operate under the influence of Satan and his kingdom.

Bondage by the enemy is not a joking matter! It's real, but the power of God is more real, and more powerful than anything the devil brings.

Although Layla had accepted the Lord Jesus Christ as Savior, everything that she had been through left a deposit of some sort in her that she needed to be delivered from. She suffered with feelings of hurt and loneliness. Many strongholds had taken over her thoughts, and dreams.

She was more entangled in the things of the devil than she actually realized, and it took a number of years before she was fully delivered from the things that she had been involved in.

When she was first saved, the Lord took away the desire to do anything ungodly. Although she had a past, and so much had to be dealt with; the Lord had changed her heart and mind. She no longer had a desire to do what she had done, go where she had been, or be who she previously was. Everything was different.

Of course, there were times when the enemy would come to tempt Layla in massive ways, but she eventually recognized a pattern. She realized that whenever she hadn't been focused-praying, fasting, and studying God's Word; the enemy would come and cause her to go back into the very things that she had been saved from. When she found herself in those positions, it wasn't because she wanted to be. She just hadn't gotten strong enough to combat the enemy and maintain the victory. In every situation, somehow the Lord always blessed her to find her way back to Him.

Deep in her heart, she was hungry for God, and she wanted Him more than anything else.

The more she learned about Him, the more she wanted Him.

She would constantly remind herself of the scripture that says; He that hungers and thirsts after righteousness, shall be filled (Matthew 5:6). Over and over again in her mind,

He that hungers and thirsts after righteousness; shall be filled! She didn't know how, or when, but she believed that it would happen.

The Lord blessed Layla to marry young and become a mother. She and her husband, once saved, made a conscious decision to raise their children to love God. They both had been in the world and they knew that the world had nothing good to offer anyone.

Before marrying, the two of them participated in a number of ungodly things, including drinking, smoking, and fornication. However no matter what they did, and how far they went, the Lord had a way of getting their attention. Right in the midst of all that they were doing, the Lord began to deal with Layla in a mighty way.

She was sitting at her desk working one day when she felt a very strong conviction come over her. She began to reflect on her life. She began to think about all the stuff that she was doing, and how far she had gotten from God once again. She became very sorrowful, and began to realize that God had been so good to her; and it wasn't just for her to throw it down the drain. She began to come to grips with the fact that the life she was living was not the life that God had for her.

Layla made up her mind that day to get things right with God.

She didn't know what that would mean for her and her fiancé at the time, but that was the least of her concerns. She just wanted to be in right relationship with God.

She began detoxing from the lifestyle, ending all behavior that she knew was wrong. A couple of weeks later, she and her fiancé were invited to attend church one Sunday morning. They accepted in the invitation, and the two of them attended the service together.

The service was good, and they both seemed to be enjoying themselves. The time had come for the alter call, and Layla had no idea what was about to take place. When the invitation for discipleship was extended, Layla's fiancé got up and walked to the front of the church.

Layla was super amazed by what was happening, she didn't waste any time. She got up and followed him. She knew that the moment she was waiting for had come. They both asked God for forgiveness that day and began to walk with the Lord all they knew how. Yes they had a long way to go, but they were ready and willing to live for God. They wanted to be saved, and saved for real.

Although they were already living together, they abstained from all sexual activity, and made the decision to move the wedding date up. They planned their wedding, and within two weeks they were married with the help of the church that they were attending. It wasn't a big elaborate wedding, but it was just enough for them, and they were so grateful.

She and her husband agreed that the life they previously lived was not the life that they wanted for their children. Layla decided that the circumstances she fell prey to, would not be an issue or burden that she would pass on to their children.

Before that day of rededication had come, the Lord was dealing with Layla intensely. She had been doing what she wanted, when she wanted, because she was grown and felt that she didn't have to answer to anyone. She knew the voice of God, but she was avoiding and ignoring God's call to draw nigh unto Him.

The Bible says in James 4:7-8, submit your selves therefore to God. Resist the devil, and he will flee from you. Draw nigh to God, and he will draw nigh to you. Cleanse your hands, ye sinners; and purify your hearts, ye double minded.

There was a tug of war going on in Layla's mind. The enemy was not turning her loose without a fight. It took determination, focus, and perseverance. It took obedience, yielding to the Holy Spirit, and discipline.

Layla had to fight. She had to fight like never before. Not a fist fight of course; but something much deeper, a spiritual fight. It was a fight for her soul. She recognized that even though she was going to church, and she was involved with the things of the church, there was still something missing. Something still seemed wrong.

She kept doing what she knew to do, but she realized that she needed help. It was imperative that she kept pushing until help came though. She just kept going and feeling her way through until she knew enough to know that complete deliverance needed to take place.

All along God was positioning Layla for deliverance. She just wasn't able to clearly see what He was doing.

One evening she was attending a powerful women's convention service, and the woman of God that brought the message that night had a mighty Word from the Lord! The message had a lot to do with being in right relationship with God and making a decision to do as the Lord says; in order to be where God desires His people to be.

That particular evening Layla was singing in the choir. The choir stayed in position during the message, and was sitting behind the pulpit.

The power of God swept through the building in an awesome way, and people were being touched, blessed, and set free. Layla lifted her hands in adoration to God, and began to worship Him for what was taking place in the house. She then extended her arms as high as they would go, closed her eyes, and enjoyed basking in the yoke breaking presence of God.

Isaiah 10:27...And it shall come to pass in that day, that his burden shall be taken away from off thy shoulder, and his yoke from off thy neck, and the yoke shall be destroyed because of the anointing.

When she closed her eyes; she shut everybody and everything else out. It was just her and God- no distractions.

She opened her mouth and began to tell God yes. She began to say,

"Your Will be done, not my will, but Thy Will be done!

Yes Lord, Yes Lord, Yes Lord!"

After a while, she could hear the Lord loud and clear.

She heard Him simply say, "Fast every day until three p.m., until I tell you to stop." Layla knew that this was not coming from her. She willingly said, "Yes Lord!"

She left church that evening and began her assignment the very next morning. She fasted until three p.m., and then after three p.m. each day there was a list of things that she did not eat at all, in an effort to continue the consecration.

She didn't understand all of it, but she was willing to do whatever it took to be free. The first three days seemed to be very rough, and it felt as if she wouldn't make it. She had hunger headaches, and at times the thought of,

"Is this necessary?"

"Maybe it's just me making this up."

"Maybe God didn't actually say anything."

Every time those thoughts surfaced, she quickly dismissed them and refocused herself; remembering what God said.

It's something about when God speaks, and you know it is God. Nobody and nothing can move you from it. The enemy tried very hard, and did so much to make her doubt, but she held on.

In the middle of this time of consecration, Layla was attending a community event at her church, and there was food. It was before three p.m., but Layla was really hungry. By now, she had been fasting until three p.m. for forty days, and the enemy was just waiting to make his move.

You see, he never really left her alone. He's cunning and sneaky. He just patiently waited to catch her at a weak moment.

The smell of the food cooking was so intense that day, and she couldn't help but watch everyone else eating. She felt weak, and began to watch the clock. It was still morning. She had a long way to go, but her focus was off because all she could think about was food, and how much longer it was going to be before she could eat.

Others noticed that she hadn't eaten anything and began to ask her why she wasn't eating. No one knew that she was fasting except for her husband -of course, and a couple of close people.

It was not for everyone to know, because they would not know how to handle it.

Layla's mind became flooded with thoughts to turn her away from what God had given her to do.

She thought, "I'm so hungry, I just need something to eat right now!"

She started to pray and ask God if it would be ok for her to eat before three p.m. just this one time. She knew what God had already said, but she was looking for Him to modify or change His mind for her in that moment. It just doesn't work that way though.

It became the perfect opportunity for the enemy to disguise himself and whisper deceiving things in her ear, making it seem as if he was God.

Layla said, "I've been fasting until three p.m. for forty days now, that's got to be long enough right? I mean Jesus fasted forty days, who am I to go any longer than Him?"

She wrestled back and forth for a little while longer before she walked over to the table and asked for a hot dog. She fixed it up the way that she wanted it, said an extensive prayer to God that included asking for forgiveness if she was wrong, and then she took a bite.

Although the hot dog seemed to be one of the best hot dogs she had ever eaten in her life, she felt so convicted after that first bite. Something was happening on the inside of her that she just couldn't explain or understand.

It felt so wrong, but she ignored the feeling, and kept telling herself that it was ok. She said,

"It's just a hot dog; it can't be that bad right?" She stood there feeling this way for a little while, and then she heard the Lord clearly say, "I didn't tell you to eat that."

God had given her an assignment. She realized then that she had been tricked by the enemy, for a hot dog. Ashamed and filled with feelings of defeat, she dropped her head in disgust.

She already knew that this time of fasting was bringing healing and deliverance. However, she was afraid that the temptation from the devil; may have just ruined all that had already been done.

Layla began to repent. She said, "Please God, give me another opportunity."

"I am so sorry for letting the enemy deceive me in a brief moment of weakness.

The Lord forgave her, and she got right back to the assignment, continuing on for a little over a year.

During that time of fasting, she stayed before the Lord in what some would call -anytime prayer. Whenever she felt a nudge from the Lord, she moved to a solitary place and prayed. She read and studied the Word of God diligently, and she followed His commands.

Others may have wanted her to go shopping with them, or watch a movie, or even sometimes just talk, but the Lord would be nudging her to study and to pray. She looked and prayed for opportunities to spend sweet quality time with the Lord, and He granted her request every time.

Because of her diligence, God was destroying the yoke of bondage that had been placed on her life. He was taking out everything that the enemy had deposited in her, and was replacing it with His love, joy, strength, and peace. He was positioning her for complete deliverance.

> *Psalm 34:17-18….The righteous cry, and*
> *the* LORD *heareth, and delivereth them*
> *out of all their troubles. The* LORD *is nigh*
> *unto them that are of a broken heart; and*
> *saveth such as be of a contrite spirit.*

She walked with the Lord, and enjoyed an intimate relationship with Him that was sweeter than anything she had ever experienced in her entire life. Complete deliverance was taking place in her. Nothing and nobody could do that, but God.

The worldly desires that she once longed to indulge in were gone, the thoughts of suicide and violence were gone, the hateful heart that she once possessed was turned into a heart of love, and she was free! She was free in her mind, free in her heart, and free to grow and do all that God had created her to do.

> *John 8:36 KJV....If the Son therefore shall make you free, ye shall be free indeed.*

God was there all along -willing to deliver, but Layla had to want it bad enough. He allowed her to get to a place where she was willing to work for it. Why? Because in working for it, she would appreciate it more. She would hold on to it, protect it, and continue the fight to keep it. She would be reminded of where she was, and what it took for her to be free.

Deliverance is something that a person fights to keep daily. She learned how important it is to fast and pray, but more importantly, she learned the fruitful benefits of being consecrated before God every day. Not just when it was convenient, or an emergency situation; but every day.

God loves when His people commune with Him. He wants to have an intimate relationship with all of His children.

> *James 4:8....Draw nigh to God, and he will draw nigh to you.*

Yes, the enemy will continue to fight, and present things that he knows has gotten a person away from God before. That's why someone that has been delivered from anything, has to watch and pray always, lest they fall into temptation and return to what they were once delivered from. Layla had to stay focused so that she wouldn't be entangled again with the yoke of bondage

Galatians 5:1…Stand fast therefore in the liberty wherewith Christ hath made us free, and be not entangled again with the yoke of bondage.

<u>Author's Note:</u> I pray that you'll remember others that you may know or suspect are suffering with some of the same experiences as Layla, and pray for them. Ask God how you can help, if only it's getting them a copy of this book to let them know God is real! Salvation and deliverance are real also, and they too can live free from the bondage of Satan!

LETTER TO THE READER

While reading this book you may have been thinking, "This sounds just like my life, or the life of someone that I know."

Perhaps, just like Layla, you have gone through a number of things that broke you down, made you afraid, and caused you to be entangled with all kinds of wicked behavior.

Just as Layla felt like there was no way out, you may feel that there is no way out, and there is no hope. But I'm writing to encourage you. There is a way out and there is hope, no matter what situation you may find yourself in. God delivered Layla and He will deliver you and/or that person that's on your heart. You simply have to repent for all of your sins. Confess that Jesus is Lord, believe in your heart that He died on the cross and God raised Him from the dead in three days, and you shall be saved! (Romans 10:9)

Now Jesus is sitting on the right hand of God, making intercession for you- for us! (Romans 8:34) He's talking to God, pleading with God for us. He loves us just that much. Yes, it's amazing- I know!

If you make the step, and give your life to God; He will change you, rearrange you, fix you, deliver you, heal you, and set you free! Just as He was and is for Layla; He will be your protection, your friend, your joy, your strength, your peace, and your love.

You will no longer have to feel lonely. He will never leave you or forsake you. (Deuteronomy 31:6)

With God you will never have to be afraid, because He will be your shield and buckler. (Psalm 91:4)

With God you will never have to feel unwanted, abandoned, abused, or unloved. He will pursue you relentlessly with His love, just as a husband pursues his wife- the love of his life.

You are the apple of God's eye and He will use you for great and mighty works in His Kingdom!

You must know and understand that God loves you. Again I stress that He loves you more than you could ever imagine. Up until now, it may have seemed like, and even felt like you were all alone. You may have felt like God doesn't care just like nobody else cares, but that's not true. That's not true at all!

I know that you may be wondering "If God cares; why did He allow all of this stuff to happen to me?"

"Why did I have to be the one?"

God allowed the struggle so that He can get the glory out of your life. What you've been through was not a mistake.

God has great work for you!

Please understand, the greater the struggle, the greater the glory. Not glory to you, but glory to God! What an honor to be chosen in such a way by God. Take comfort in knowing that His strength is made perfect in your weakness. (2 Corinthians 12:9)

You have to make a decision.

Knowing now that everything you've been through was not a mistake or for naught; what are you going to do with all of the wisdom, knowledge, and experience that you've gained? Must you hold it all in and keep it to yourself? Prayerfully not!

That's not God's purpose for allowing you to go through it. Be willing to use what you have to help someone else along the way.

Believe it or not, there are millions of people that need you. They are waiting on someone like you to help them out of whatever situation they are in. They are waiting to hear that they are not alone. They are waiting to hear that there is hope and freedom in Jesus! What good is your experience if you don't put it to use?

Think of it as a high school diploma or a college degree. A person that goes through school, enduring every obstacle that arises, and perseveres to graduation obtains something that will not only be helpful to them, but also be helpful to others.

That college degree shows that you endured through whatever it took, and you've gained knowledge along with a certain level of expertise in a specific area. Now you are in a position to use what you've learned to help someone else. When you go out to apply for a specific job, that degree is what qualifies you for the position.

So it is with what you've gone through in life. Your struggle has qualified you for a specific assignment. Again, God wants to use you for great and mighty things!

Just surrender your life, your thoughts, your plans, and your will to Him. Then trust Him with all of it. Be sure that you are under good leadership that will train you. You need leaders that will help you to grow and mature in Christ; leaders that are able to help you get to where God is calling you to. The right Godly leaders are essential for your specific purpose.

I can't stress this enough, you are chosen by God! Don't sit in discouragement, depression, and defeat. Get up and go on, walking in what God has called and qualified you for. It's a process, and it takes time, but if you keep going; you're going to make it. God's grace is sufficient for you!

I love you, and I'm praying for you!

Love,
Sister Megan Walker

Follow the Author

Website/Blog:
www.mgisnovel.com

E-Mail:
mygraceissufficient.mwalker@gmail.com

Facebook:
fb.me/mygraceissufficient.mwalker

Pinterest:
www.pinterest.com/mygraceissufficientmwalker

Printed in the United States
By Bookmasters